I'm Polite but I Know My Traffic Light

A CHILD'S GUIDE FOR LISTENING TO THEIR INTUITION

Jennifer Becker
Illustrator: Pandu Permana

I'm Polite but I Know My Traffic Light
Copyright © 2022 by Jennifer Becker

Tellwell Talent
www.tellwell.ca

ISBN
978-0-2288-7701-1 (Paperback)

Hi my name is Sally and I'm 8 years old. I'm learning about how to politely answer when I'm asked to do things!

When I'm asked to do something that I feel happy and excited about then I know I have a green light. Yippee!!!

Sometimes when I'm asked to do things I feel confused or a bit unsure, that's when I talk to my parents or someone older who I trust, I call this my yellow light!

When I'm asked to do something that makes me feel all yucky in my tummy, that's when I know I have a red light. I don't do things that make me feel all icky yucky yuck and I always tell an adult right away.

Green light means,
go, go, go!

Yellow light means,
careful and slow!

Red light means,
stop and find
a safe place to go!

The other day my mom asked me to make a birthday card for my grandma. I felt excited and I said "yes"! In my head I could see a big green light! As I made the card, I felt joy in my heart because I knew my grandma would just LOVE it!!!

Happy Birthday Grandma!

I used lots of sparkles and the color purple, because that's my grandma's favorite color!

Happy Birthday Grandma!

When I handed my grandma the card, she had a big smile and she said it was beautiful and she put it on her shelf. I was proud of myself for making her a birthday card!

We had fun at my grandma's party, we sang and laughed and played with balloons.

When we were leaving my uncle called me over and asked for a hug. I like my uncle, he's so funny and is always telling jokes!

But I didn't really want to give him a hug, and I felt a bit confused. I saw a yellow light in my head so I asked my dad what I should do. My dad said, "Why don't you give Uncle a high 5?" I love giving Uncle high 5's so I said yes! Uncle said, "Down low, too slow", and pulled his hand away, it made me laugh! I like asking someone for help when I see a yellow light and I'm not sure what to do!

When we got home from my grandma's house
I was so tired, what a fun day!

I was getting ready for bed, and my older brother's

friend came in my bedroom and said he wanted to lay

beside me in my bed. I love playing video games with

him, but I didn't want him to lay with me in my bed,

that made me feel icky yucky yuck in my tummy, so I said,

"please don't lay in my bed". I could see a red light in my

head and I knew something wasn't right.

I went and told my parents right away because I knew I would feel better if I talked about it. They were proud of me and I was proud of me too!

During the night Jane's cousins came into the house and

they were yelling at each other and doing things that

seemed scary! I heard a little voice in my head saying,

it's time to LEAVE.

I nicely asked to use the phone and called my dad, who

came quickly to pick me up. My parents were happy

that I decided to come home when I didn't feel safe.

I saw a red light and got to a safe place,

I had a good sleep in my own bed!

Ted talked to his auntie and she suggested for him to bring along his older brother, Charlie. Mr. Harold, Ted and Charlie went boating for the day and they had so much fun!

My friend Ted is super-duper smart, he always makes good choices!

Ted also loves to play hockey and he's one of the best players on his team! He scores lots of goals YAHOO!

One day Ted's hockey coach ended the practice early.

He whispered to Ted to come over to his house for a

private extra practice. Ted felt icky yuck yuck in his tummy, he

said "no thanks". Ted called his parents right away.

Ted saw a red light and got to a safe place, YAY Ted!!

You get my special gold star!

Always remember:

Green light means, go, go, go!

Yellow light means, careful and slow!

**Red light means, stop
and find a safe place to go!**

The other day, our teacher asked Ted and a couple other students to stay in the classroom during recess to clean our class pet's cage.

We have the cutest little hamster named Fluffy. Ted thought about it and said, "sure I would be happy to clean Fluffy's cage"!

Ted saw a green light in his head because his friends were staying with him to help.

It makes Ted feel good to lend a helping hand. Ted and his friends kept laughing at Fluffy because she was running a million miles a minute in her hamster ball! Silly Fluffy!!

When a new park opened my dad asked Carrie if she wanted to come to the park with us.

Carrie saw a big green light in her head,

it was an easy choice for her to make!

She said, "yes please"!!!

She felt excited, especially because there's

a really awesome zipline that is so high

it almost touches the sky! We love the new park

and stayed there almost all day!

Carrie told me that last week when she finished gym

class her teacher asked her to stay behind after her friends

left. He told her to come into the equipment room and

said that he had a secret to tell her.

Even though he's Carrie's favourite teacher, she

heard a little voice in her head telling her not to go

into the room alone with him and she saw a yellow

light in her head.

Carrie told her teacher that she needed to use the washroom. She went and talked to her homeroom teacher about it since she was a little unsure what to do. Carrie did the right thing, she didn't feel comfortable, so she left.

Her mom was proud of her too!! My friend Carrie is probably one of the smartest friends I have, I call her my savvy bestie!

Let's practice the traffic lights one more time
Just like I do with friends of mine!

Green light means, go, go, go!

Yellow light means,
careful and slow!

Red light means,
stop and find
a safe place to go!

When I have yellow or red lights, I always talk to someone I trust.

In my life, I mostly get green lights and sometimes yellow,

but when I feel scared or get an icky yucky yuck feeling in my

tummy then I know I have a red light. I can say "no"

and get to a safe place.

I'm so glad that my friends know their traffic lights

too and now so do you!! You can practice everyday!

Hip Hip Hooray!

I'm Polite, but I know My Traffic Light

Activity Sheet

Remember your traffic light to help keep yourself safe:

Green light means, go, go, go!
Feelings I have with a green light

_____

Yellow light means, careful and slow!
Feelings I have with a yellow light

_____

Red light means, stop and find a safe place to go! Feelings I have with a red light

_____

These are people I trust who I can talk to when I have a yellow or red light:

_____

Manufactured by Amazon.ca
Acheson, AB

11492962R00021